This igloo book belongs to:

igloobooks

Published in 2017
by Igloo Books Ltd
Cottage Farm
Sywell
NN6 0BJ
www.igloobooks.com

Original tales retold by Sienna Williams

Illustrated by Gail Yerrill
Additional colour by Kim Fleming, Xenia Pavlova,
Iole Eulalia Rosa, Pauline Siewert and Nicky Storr

Designed by Kerri-Ann Hulme
Edited by Stephanie Moss

HUN001 0717
2 4 6 8 10 9 7 5 3 1
ISBN 978-1-78670-717-8

Printed and manufactured in China

The
Snow Queen
and Other Stories

igloobooks

Contents

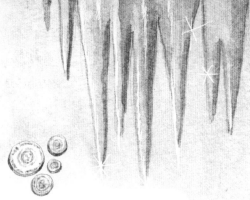

Hans Christian Andersen

The Snow Queen

Once upon a time, there was a wicked sorcerer who created an enchanted mirror. It had the power to stop people from seeing anything joyful and happy, so anyone who looked into it saw only the bad things in the world. Eventually, their hearts became cold and cruel and this pleased the terrible sorcerer.

One day, the sorcerer was so filled with pride because of his enchanted mirror that he flew up to the sky, laughing. In fact, he laughed so much, that the magic mirror slipped from his hands, and when he dropped it, the mirror fell to Earth. It shattered into millions of tiny pieces that were carried off by the wind and blown across the world, like snowflakes in a swirling snowstorm.

The great wind, carrying pieces of the enchanted mirror, blew and settled in a pretty little town. Two friends called Kai and Gerda lived there and they loved one another just as much as a brother and sister. When it was warm, Gerda and Kai loved playing in the rose gardens.

When winter came, they listened to stories and legends about the Snow Queen. It was said that her cape was like a million starry snowflakes, but her icy touch would freeze even the warmest heart.

One day, Kai looked up
to the sky and laughed
at the silly tales of the
legendary queen.

Suddenly, a tiny splinter of the
magic mirror fell into his eye
and another pierced his heart.

As if his heart had turned to ice, Kai instantly
became cold and cruel. "I'm not playing with a
silly girl," he said to Gerda and ran off to play with
the older boys. Gerda cried, as she watched Kai
whispering and laughing at her with his new friends.

Soon after, a magical, glittering sleigh swept into the town. The woman inside had eyes that glittered like cold, twinkling diamonds. Her cape was made from snow and her crown was made of ice. It was the Snow Queen, who Kai and Gerda had heard tales of for so long.

No sooner had she arrived and thick snowflakes began to fall, than she leapt out of her sleigh and wrapped Kai in her icy embrace. Then, she drove out of town, into the long, winter night.

Gerda waited until spring for Kai to come back to their little town, but he did not return. As she sat beside the river, crying, she saw a small boat. She climbed carefully into it and floated down the river, hoping to find him.

On and on the little boat floated, past woods and meadows, until it came to rest by a magical flower garden. "Hello, child," said an old woman, greeting Gerda outside her cottage, nearby. The scent from the magical flowers was so sweet that Gerda soon forgot all about Kai.

Gerda stayed in the cottage, then, one day, in the furthest corner of the garden, she found a single pretty rose. Suddenly, she remembered Kai and began to cry.
"He is not gone," whispered the rose.
"I must find him," said Gerda and she ran off at once into the dark wood.

Gerda ran until her feet ached.
"I wish I could find Kai," she said, sadly. Then, a crow flapped his wings above her.
"There was a boy who came to a palace near here," cawed the crow.

Gerda was sure that the boy the bird spoke of must be Kai, so the crow took Gerda to an elegant palace nearby. To her disappointment, she did not find him there. Instead, she met a kind prince and princess. "You poor child," they said, as Gerda told them her story, sadly. "You must stay the night with us."

In the morning, the prince and
princess dressed Gerda in the finest
silk and velvet. Then, they sent her on
her way in an enchanted golden coach.
"We hope you find your friend," they called, as they
waved goodbye. The little coach rattled over pebbles and
stones on the winding forest path. It had not gone far when
a band of robbers jumped out and attacked the golden carriage.

That night, at the robber's camp, a little robber-girl watched Gerda, as she sat with her reindeer by her side. The robber-girl felt sorry for Gerda, as she looked frightened and seemed to be all alone. "Don't cry," she told Gerda, hugging her and listening to her tale.

The robber-girl decided to show Gerda all of her little animals to cheer her up. Soon, they came across a pigeon who spoke of Kai. "Where was he going?" asked Gerda, desperately. The pigeon told her he was travelling with the Snow Queen to Lapland.

So, when all the robbers were asleep, the kind robber-girl put Gerda on her reindeer. "Go and find the Lapland woman," she whispered. "She will tell you how to find the Snow Queen."

Through snowstorms and fierce winds, Gerda rode on the reindeer to the frozen plains where the Lapland woman lived. "You poor things," she said, when they reached her little hut. "You have a long way to go yet. You must go to see the Finland woman," said the Lapland woman. "She can tell you more about the Snow Queen!"

On and on went Gerda and the reindeer. Then, inside a warm, strangely decorated hut, Gerda found the Finland woman. "What you seek is within your reach," said the woman. Gerda was overjoyed. "Your friend is not dead, but he is enchanted by a splinter from a magic mirror and his heart is as cold as ice. Only your love can save him. You must travel to where the Northern Lights are brightest and there you will find the palace of the Snow Queen."

Finally, Gerda reached the palace of the Snow Queen. Its great ice walls glittered coldly and its empty halls were silent. In the middle of a cracked and frozen lake, Gerda found Kai. His cheeks were blue with cold and the Snow Queen was by his side. As she bent down to give him the final kiss that would turn him to ice once and for all, Gerda cried out to him, "No!" A trickle of warm tears ran down Gerda's cheeks onto Kai's frozen skin and the splinter that had lodged in his heart was washed away.

"I've missed you, Gerda," said Kai,
hugging her. Kai began to cry and, as he
did, the splinter of glass washed from his eye,
freeing him from the evil of the mirror. The Snow
Queen's eyes flashed angrily, as she saw them together.
"The strength of your love is no match for me," she cried.
With that, she whirled around and was gone, like a snowflake
melting on a warm summer's day. From then on, Kai and Gerda's
friendship was stronger than ever. They returned to their town, where
they enjoyed every day like it was the first one of spring.

Hans Christian Andersen

The Little Tin Soldier

There once was a little boy who had a box of little toy soldiers. They all wore smart red and blue uniforms and held rifles over their shoulders. All of them had been made from just one old tin spoon and were exactly the same, except for one very special little tin soldier. There had not been enough tin to finish him after the others were made, so he only had one leg to stand on. "I like you best," whispered the little boy, as he lined him up with the others.

There was also a pretty palace made of paper in the little boy's playroom. It had tall turrets and a lake made of glass, with elegant swans swimming on it. Dancing in the doorway was a beautiful paper ballerina. She stood gracefully on one leg, with her arms above her. Her other leg was hidden under her tutu, so from where the little one-legged tin soldier stood, she looked just like him.

What the little boy didn't know was, when no one else was around, all of his toys came to life! "The ballerina is so pretty and graceful," thought the little tin soldier, "and she has only one leg, just like me!"

He felt blissfully happy. "I'm not so different after all," he thought, standing up taller and straighter than ever. "The ballerina and I are meant for each other." The little tin soldier had fallen deeply in love.

When the little boy went to bed, all of the toys in the playroom started having fun, as they did each night. "Catch!" said the teddies, bouncing their ball. "Duck!" said the jesters, playing leapfrog, but the tin soldier only had eyes for the ballerina.

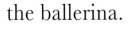

All of a sudden, the jack-in-the-box popped up with a BOING! and pointed at the little tin soldier. "Do not wish for things that are out of your reach," he warned, "or something bad might happen." The little tin soldier pretended not to hear him.

27

The next day, the little boy moved the soldiers off the table and stood them on the big, wide windowsill where the sun made their uniforms look brighter than ever. He began marching them up and down, saying, "Left, right! Left, right!" Suddenly, a strong gust of wind blew the window open and the little one-legged soldier fell out onto the street below.

He landed with a BUMP! in a pile of soft, crunchy leaves, but the little tin soldier knew how important it was to be brave, so he didn't call out for help. Suddenly, as he felt big, wet raindrops splashing on his face, two children stumbled upon him. "Look," said one, picking him up, "let's make a boat for him!" So, they made a little boat out of newspaper and placed the soldier carefully inside, before sailing it down the gutter with him in it.

"I must be brave," thought the little tin soldier, as the paper boat rushed along the stream in the gutter, going faster and faster.

All at once, there was a WHOOSH! as the boat carried the soldier into a drain and everything went dark.

"Where am I going now?" he wondered. "I wouldn't care if it was twice as dark, if only I could have the beautiful ballerina sailing with me."

Just then, the soldier heard a scurrying, followed by a SPLASH! A huge water rat that lived in the drain paddled over to the little boat. The little tin soldier felt very scared, but he didn't say a word. "This is no place for tin soldiers," snarled the rat. "Show me your passport!" he demanded. The soldier was silent and the boat sailed on, but the rat followed, gnashing his teeth and crying out, "Stop him, stop him!"

With the rat's cries echoing behind him, the little tin soldier's heart leapt for joy, as he saw daylight ahead of him. Then, he heard a rushing, roaring noise. "Oh, no!" cried the little tin soldier. He saw that where the tunnel ended, the drain fell into a great big river. "If I am carried down the waterfall," he said, "my little paper boat is sure to sink!"

The paper boat was now so near to the edge that the little tin soldier couldn't stop. "I must be brave!" he repeated, as the water in the gutter shot out into the river, taking the boat and the little tin soldier with it.

The paper boat was sucked into a swirling, gurgling whirlpool, where it whirled round and round.

The little paper boat got wetter and wetter and before long, it was full to the brim with river water.

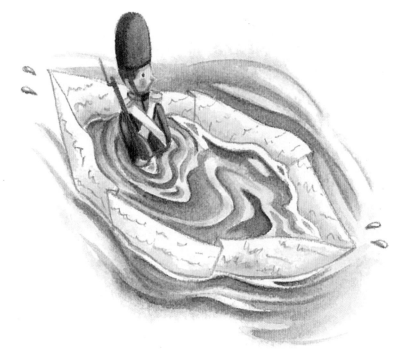

The little tin soldier stood up to his waist in water and cried out, "Oh, dear!" as the paper grew softer and softer and the boat began to sink.

Finally, the paper boat broke in half and the little tin soldier could no longer stand in it.

"I will never see the ballerina again!" thought the little tin soldier, as he floated down and down. Just as he was about to sink all the way to the bottom, still clutching his rifle and standing as brave and proud as ever, a great big fish noticed his bright red and blue uniform.

"That looks like it might be nice to eat," thought the fish, and he opened his mouth for the little tin soldier to float inside.

Luckily, the little boy that the tin soldier belonged to was fishing by the very same river. He reeled in his line and hooked the soldier out of the fish's mouth.

"How did you get all the way out here?" he wondered. "I'm going to take you home to join the others." Safe and sound at last, the soldier couldn't wait to see his beloved ballerina once more.

Back in the playroom, the little one-legged tin soldier thought the ballerina looked as beautiful as ever. As the little boy lined him back up with the others, his sister came in to play with him. "I think that soldier wants to be with the paper ballerina," she said, and she stood him beside her. The little tin soldier had never felt such happiness. He gazed at the ballerina with love in his heart and she gazed back at him, happy together at last.

~ Hans Christian Andersen ~

The Princess and the Pea

Once upon a time, there was a handsome prince who lived in a royal kingdom. More than anything in the world, he wanted to find a real princess to marry, so he could make her his queen.

The prince travelled far and wide and met lots of beautiful maidens from many different lands, but none of them were ever exactly what he was looking for.

"She appears to be a princess," the prince would think to himself each time, "but something doesn't seem quite right."

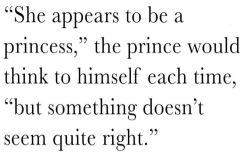

Feeling very downhearted and weary from travelling, the disappointed prince returned home to the royal palace. He sat by the window of his lonely tower, wishing that there was a way that he could find the perfect princess to marry.

Then, one dark night, a terrible storm raged across the kingdom. Lightning bolts flashed across the sky and thunder boomed, as the wind howled and wailed. Rain clattered and battered against the windowpanes and ran in droplets down the drenched rooftops.

Suddenly, as the king watched the storm through his window, he saw someone running towards the palace. "Who could possibly be out on such a night?" wondered the king, as he opened the door to find out who it was.

To the king's surprise, he saw a beautiful girl, standing on the doorstep. "Good heavens," he said, sounding very startled, as the mysterious girl was completely soaking wet. In fact, the wind and the rain made her look as though she had just climbed out of the palace river! The water ran down from her hair and clothes, trickled into her shoes and spilled onto the palace floor into little puddles all around her. She smiled, shyly, shivering.

"I beg your pardon for calling so late," said the girl, "but I have come to ask you to help me. I am a princess from another land and I am lost in this terrible storm. Please, will you give me shelter for the night?" The king did not hesitate for a moment. "Of course," he said. "Come in, my dear."

Nearby, the queen was listening. "Surely this girl can't be a real princess?" she thought. The queen wanted nothing more than for her son to find happiness with a bride, but if it was to be with this mysterious girl, she must know if she truly was a princess. "There's only one way to find out," the queen whispered to herself, as she tiptoed upstairs to one of the royal bedchambers.

"Put this single pea on the base of this bed," the queen commanded her servants, "then lay twenty mattresses on top of it."

One by one, the mattresses were stacked on the pea. What a job the servants had! At last, the task was complete and it was time for everyone to go to bed.

47

In the morning, the king and queen came to the girl's bedchamber to ask how she had slept.

"Oh, I slept very badly!" replied the girl. "I tossed and turned all night and hardly closed my eyes."

"The bed looked so very comfortable, but it felt like I was lying on something hard. I may as well have been sleeping on a stone!"

The queen was very happy. "I can't believe it!" she whispered to the king. "Only a true princess could have felt a single pea beneath twenty soft mattresses." It seemed that her son might find a wife after all. So, she rushed up to the prince's tower to introduce him to the beautiful princess.

When the prince laid eyes on the princess, he fell instantly in love her, and she with him. He was very happy because at last he had found a true princess. Soon after, the prince married the princess and they lived happily ever after.

The king and the queen were very happy, too. After many years of searching, their only son had found a wife. They no longer needed the pea, but because it had been so useful, they decided to put it into a museum and as far as anyone knows, it is still there to this very day.

Hans Christian Andersen

The Wild Swans

Once upon a time, there was a noble and patient king. He had eleven kind sons and one beautiful daughter, named Eliza. They lived in a grand palace and were very happy together, but when the king remarried, everything changed. The new queen was a wicked woman, but most of all, she was jealous and couldn't bear to see how happy the king was with his children.

So one morning, when the king was hunting and Eliza was still fast asleep, the evil queen cast a spell on the eleven princes. "Fly away, great birds, fly away!" she screeched. Instead of them turning into ugly birds as she had wished, the princes turned into eleven beautiful, wild swans, right before her eyes. Then, they beat their wings and flew away from the palace, each calling out a strange cry.

"Where are my sons?" the king asked when he returned. The queen simply replied that they had left because they didn't love him. Heartbroken and betrayed, the king allowed the queen to send Eliza away from the palace, to live with a family of peasants in the country. "Please, Father, no," pleaded the princess, as tears streamed down her face, but the king turned away from his only daughter.

As she began her new life in the country, Eliza missed her brothers terribly. One evening, as she was walking in the forest, she came across a wise-looking old woman. "If you follow the river," she told Eliza, "you might just find what you're looking for."

Sure enough, when she reached the water's edge, Eliza looked up at the setting sun. Suddenly, eleven swans appeared in the sky, each wearing a golden crown.

The swans landed in a circle around Eliza and she threw her arms round their long necks. She recognised her brothers instantly!

Then, as the sun slipped behind the horizon, they transformed and became human once more. "Hello, brothers!" cried Eliza, feeling overjoyed.

"We only have until the morning," they told her, sadly.
"The queen's spell turns us back into swans at sunrise every day."

Eliza and her brothers stayed up long into the night, talking.
"You cannot stay here," the princes told her. "We must take you back
to our beautiful new home, across the sea." So, her brothers began
weaving a net of willow and reeds, which Eliza lay down and slept upon.
"This will surely be strong enough," said the eldest, at dawn, just as they
all turned back into their majestic bird form.

With Eliza still sleeping, the swans seized the net in their great beaks and flew up into the clouds to begin their long journey home. When Eliza awoke, the bright sunbeams fell on her face, so her brothers shielded her with their great wings.

They flew over hills and valleys, fields and rivers, until they finally landed at a rocky, hillside cave. "This is your new home," they told Eliza.

That night, as Eliza fell asleep on a bed of soft, white swans' feathers, she longed to break the queen's evil spell. No sooner had she wished it, than a magical voice replied, "You must weave each of your brothers a shirt made of nettles, but from the moment you begin until you finish, you must not speak a word to anyone. If you do, your brothers will remain as swans forever."

Overjoyed that she could finally help her brothers, Eliza set to work. "I must gather as many nettle leaves as I can," she thought.

The sting of the nettles hurt Eliza's hands, but she began weaving them, just as the voice had told her to.

Though her hands were red and her fingers were sore, the brave and kind Eliza was silent for the sake of her brothers.

One evening, the princes visited Eliza after sunset. "What are you doing?"
they asked, seeing her weaving the nettles with her painful hands, but she could
only shake her head. "She cannot speak!" they cried. "The queen must have
cast another evil spell." Suddenly, the youngest brother began to cry and they
understood that what she was doing was all for them. As he cried, his tears fell
on Eliza's hands and she smiled, as suddenly, all of her pain disappeared.

Eliza worked through many nights without rest and quickly finished the first nettle shirt. One day, she heard the TOOT-TOOT of a hunting horn and the young king of the land found Eliza in her cave.

"What is your name?" he asked, thinking she was the most beautiful girl he had ever seen, but Eliza could only smile sweetly.

"You must come with me and live in the palace," he said, and with that, they galloped away.

At the palace, Eliza was given beautiful clothes to wear, but all she could think of was completing the nettle shirts.

The king, meanwhile, had fallen deeply in love with Eliza. "I will make her my bride," he told his advisors, but they had seen Eliza creeping out of the palace at night and did not trust her. What they did not see was that Eliza was simply gathering nettles beyond the palace walls, but of course, she could not tell anyone why.

On the day of Eliza and the king's wedding, all but one of the shirts was finished, but still, Eliza kept working. "We mustn't let the king marry her," whispered his advisors. They planned to take Eliza to him and reveal what they knew, but she was so exhausted, she could not walk. They pulled her through the courtyard in a cart, but little did they know, Eliza had the shirts with her.

Just as Eliza finished weaving the last one, there was a strange cry overhead. Eleven swans, wearing crowns on their heads, flew down and surrounded her. Eliza threw the shirts over them and instantly, the queen's spell was broken. Finally able to speak, Eliza said to the king, "These are my brothers." Then, she explained the whole story to him. They were married at once, to great celebration throughout the kingdom, but happiest of all were Eliza and her brothers, who were reunited at last.

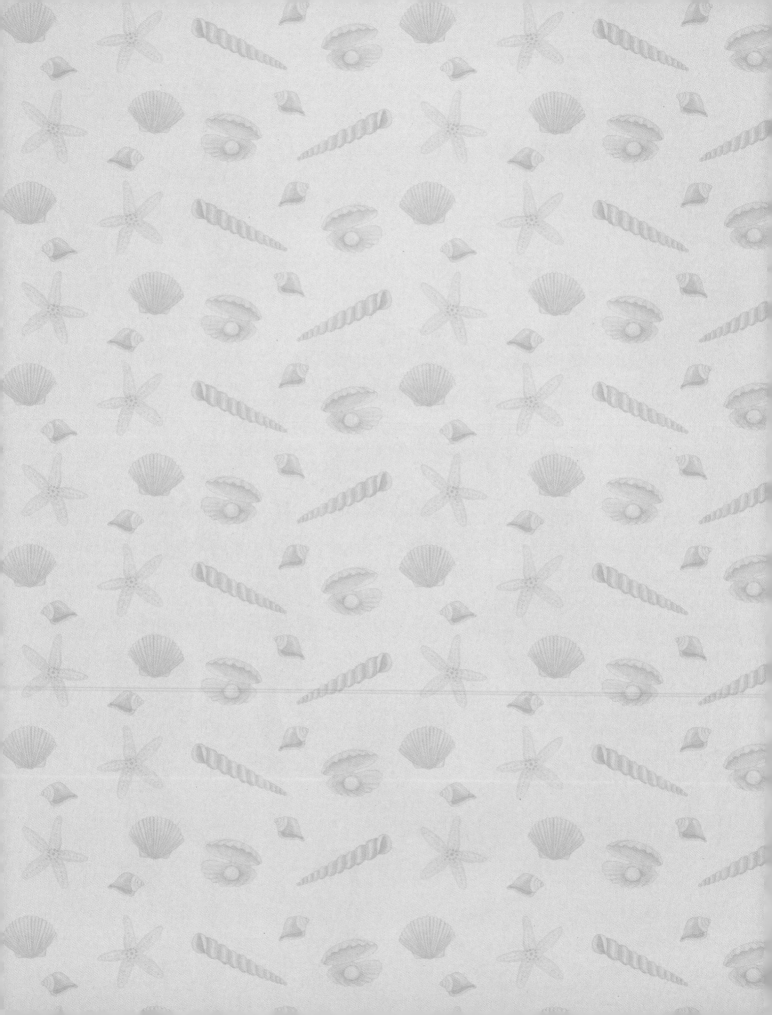

Hans Christian Andersen

The Little Mermaid

Once upon a time, there was a little mermaid who lived in a beautiful palace under the sea. All day long, she played among the bright blooms of the sea gardens, but the Little Mermaid longed for adventure. She had watched each of her older sisters before her, one by one, swim up to the water's surface and explore the world above. When they returned, she was enchanted by the amazing tales of what they saw beyond the sea.

"The water twinkles like diamonds in the sunlight," they would tell her.
"There are more shades in the sky than there are fish in the sea!" they added.
The Little Mermaid dreamed of when she too could visit the land above
the waves. Then, on her sixteenth birthday, the Sea King came
to the Little Mermaid to tell her that her time had come.
"Goodbye, everyone!" she called, as she darted
through the water to the world above.

When she reached the surface, the
Little Mermaid couldn't believe her eyes.
Everything her sisters had told her was true!
The sun was setting and the sky glowed in the
glimmering twilight. As she looked around in
wonder, she saw a ship where people
were laughing and dancing.

Swimming closer, the Little
Mermaid saw a handsome,
young prince. She could not
take her eyes off him and, as
she watched him, she fell
instantly in love.

As the hours passed, the sea became restless. The ship's sails began to billow and the waves began to rise higher and higher. Heavy clouds darkened the sky and jagged lightning flashed. Soon, a terrible storm struck and the ship creaked and groaned. Huge, crashing waves tore at the mast and ripped it in two.

The Little Mermaid watched as her beloved prince was flung into the sea and sank, helpless, beneath the cruel waves. "I must rescue him," thought the Little Mermaid, "or he will surely die."

She dived down beneath the water and pulled the prince up to the surface. Then, she swam with him to safety and held him tightly until the storm ceased. She kissed his forehead, tenderly.

"Goodbye, my prince," whispered the Little Mermaid, as she left him on the shore and swam behind some nearby rocks until he awoke.

Then, to her surprise, the Little Mermaid saw a pretty, young girl wander across the sand. She ran to the prince and, when he opened his eyes, he smiled up at the girl, as if she had been the one who had saved him from the stormy sea.

The Little Mermaid's heart sank. "If only he knew who had truly rescued him," she thought, with tears in her eyes. So, she turned and dived back below the waves.

The Little Mermaid knew she had to be with her prince again. She had heard terrible tales of the Sea Witch, but she knew only her magic could help her. She swam down into the coldest, darkest waters at the bottom of the sea and began to shiver, as she heard the Sea Witch cackle. "She must be this way," thought the Little Mermaid, making her way through the seaweed.

Sure enough, in a house made of bones, the
Little Mermaid found the Sea Witch. She told
her the story of her beloved prince and how
she wished to marry him. "Can you help me?"
asked the Little Mermaid. The Sea Witch smiled.
"Drink this potion and you will become human,"
she said. "However, in return, you must give me
your voice." The Little Mermaid agreed and
drank the potion.

No sooner had she finished the last drop, than the Little Mermaid flicked and swished her tail. "I must return to my prince," she thought, swimming up through the blue water, as she felt her tail slowly beginning to change. By the time she reached the surface, the Little Mermaid found she had two legs. She opened her mouth to gasp, but she couldn't speak. The Sea Witch had taken her voice, just as she promised.

The Little Mermaid found her way to the prince's palace, where he took pity on her, and from that day on, he treated her as if she were his own sister. "How will I ever tell him who I am and how much I love him?" she despaired each day, as he took her riding through the sweet-scented woods. Then, one day, the prince told the Little Mermaid that his father had arranged for him to marry someone else.

The very next day, the Little Mermaid and the prince sailed together to meet his new bride. In the streets, bells rang and trumpets blew. "You are the girl from the beach who rescued me," the prince said to the princess who appeared in front of him. "I have loved you since the first moment I saw you, but I never thought we would meet again!" With that, the happy prince took the princess in his arms and kissed her.

The Little Mermaid was heartbroken, for her prince would never know how much she loved him. When no one was looking, she slipped away from her true love and dived back down under the sea. As the water covered her legs, they transformed back into a silvery fishtail again. Her voice came back to her once more and she swam down, down into the water, singing her sad song, all the way to her underwater palace.

Back at home with her family, the Little Mermaid sobbed. The Sea King hugged her tightly and said, "There, there, child. Do not waste your tears on what is not meant to be. You might have been happy with the prince for a while, but your heart would have missed the ocean. You are a mermaid and your home is under the sea. You belong here, with us."

The Little Mermaid's sisters wiped away her tears and combed her hair and she was soon happy again in her underwater home. They swam with her to the surface and watched as the handsome prince and his beautiful princess were married. "Goodbye," said the Little Mermaid, sadly, diving back underneath the rippling waves.

~ Hans Christian Andersen ~

The Flying Trunk

Once upon a time, there was a rich merchant. He was so wealthy, he could have paved the streets with gold, but he never spent a penny of his fortune. When he died, his son became rich and led an expensive and luxurious life. He invited his friends to fancy parties every night and held splendid banquets in his grand mansion until soon, all the money was gone.

The merchant's son was left with nothing. His friends, who had only cared for his money, all deserted him, except for one. He sent him an old trunk so that he could pack up his things and leave town.

"What am I going to do with this?" wondered the merchant's son. He only had a pair of slippers and a dressing gown to wear. He had nothing else to pack inside a trunk.

He had nowhere to sleep, so the merchant's son decided to climb into the trunk himself, instead.

As soon as he put the key in the lock...WHOOSH! To his surprise, the trunk flew up into the sky.

"Woo-hoo!" he cried, somersaulting through the clouds. He flew over land and sea, all day and all night, until he reached a foreign place he'd never been before.

The merchant's son left the magical,
flying trunk in the woods and went
to explore the marketplace. It was
bustling with people, buying and selling
exotic wares. Suddenly, he spotted
a tall palace, high up on a hill. "Who lives up
there, in that beautiful palace?" he asked someone passing by.
"The sultan's daughter," replied the stranger. "No one is allowed
to see her without her mother and father, as it was predicted long
ago that she would be unhappy with whoever she married."

The merchant's son was determined to meet the princess, so that night, he got into his trunk and put the key in the lock. WHOOSH! He flew to the top of the palace and climbed into her window.

"She's beautiful," he whispered, as he laid eyes on the princess while she slept, but the sound of his voice woke her up.

"Who are you?" she asked, feeling confused.

"I'm an angel," said the merchant's son. "I've flown through the sky just to see you." The princess liked the sound of that and so he spent the whole night telling her stories about her beauty. By morning, the princess had fallen in love with the merchant's son and when he asked her to marry him, she agreed right away.

As the merchant's son went to leave, the princess hesitated. "Come back next week and see my parents, but be sure to have a story to tell," she said, "or they will forbid our marriage." She knew her mother and father would be impressed to meet an angel, but he would have to tell a funny story for the sultan, and it wouldn't please the sultan's wife without a moral.

So, the merchant's son set about dreaming up one perfect story to tell them both. The next week, he flew through the window and the princess' parents gasped. "Is this the angel you told us about?" the sultan asked his daughter. She nodded and he replied, "We can't wait to hear a funny tale."

"Though it must have a moral, too," said his wife.

"Then I will begin," said the merchant's son.

"Once upon a time," he said, "there was a box of matches that loved making up stories."

"They told everyone that they were made from a great tree that enjoyed the sunshine all day. They said that the rest of the tree had been made into a grand ship that sailed around the whole wide world."

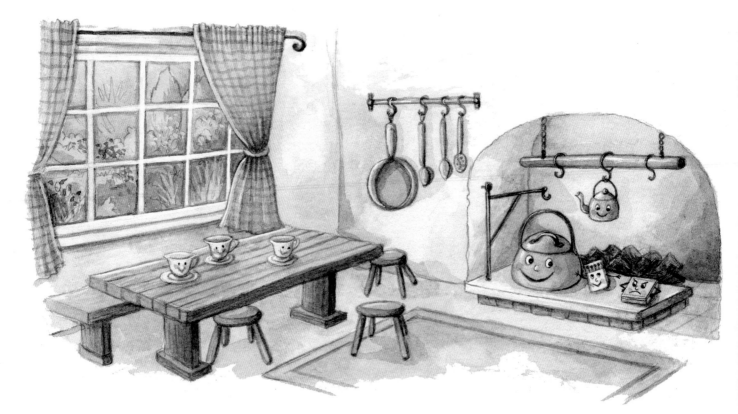

"The pot, the kettle and the teacups all wished they'd had as many adventures as the matches," said the merchant's son.

"The tinderbox wasn't impressed," he continued. "He thought the matches should be happy with who they really were, instead of telling tales."

"Then, a servant came into the kitchen and chose the matches to light the fire."

"They were so pleased at how they shined and impressed everyone, but of course in the end, they burned out and were gone forever."

The sultan and his wife loved his story. "You shall marry our daughter tomorrow!" they cried, and the whole city celebrated, dancing and singing in the streets. "I must impress the people before I marry the princess," thought the merchant's son, so he bought fireworks of every kind.

POP! went the crackers. BANG! went the rockets, as the merchant's son flew through the sky in his trunk, setting them off.

"Oh, no!" he cried, after the celebrations. "A spark from the fireworks has burned my trunk to ashes!" All because he had tried to impress everyone, his flying trunk was gone forever. The princess waited for him in her tower on their wedding day, but he had no way to reach her.

From that day on, the merchant's son travelled the world telling stories, each one with a great moral, and he promised never to boast to anyone ever again.

~ Hans Christian Andersen ~

The Ugly Duckling

One summer, long ago, when the golden corn had ripened in the fields, a mother duck settled down by the riverbank on her nest of eggs.

She sat, very patiently, until suddenly, she heard a noise. TAP, TAP, TAP!

One of the egg shells began to crack, then another and another.

Soon, one by one, tiny heads poked out. PEEP-PEEP, QUACK-QUACK! went the little ducklings, as they looked around.

Soon, all of the eggs had hatched, except for one. This egg was much larger than the others. "Maybe it's a turkey egg," thought the mother duck, settling back down to keep it warm. Some time later, there was a soft, cracking sound. It got louder and louder until suddenly, a fluffy head poked out of the egg, then a body. This duckling was not at all like the others. It was very large, grey and ugly.

"Maybe it is a turkey after all," said the mother duck. "Let's see if it can swim." She watched as, one after another, the ducklings plopped into the water with a SPLASH! The ducklings had a lovely time practising their swimming. They dived, quacked and splashed, but the little grey duckling hid shyly in the reeds.

So, the mother duck decided that it was time for them all to meet the animals in the farmyard. "I shall see what they think of my new family," she thought and she waddled up the bank, with all the ducklings following behind her.

In the farmyard, the hens and geese looked at the new arrivals. "What's that one at the end?" they cried, laughing. "He looks so ugly!" The other farm animals all gathered round. They too thought the duckling was very ugly. They didn't like him at all. From then on, the poor little duckling was pushed, bitten and made fun of.

After a while, his brothers and sisters began to bully him and even his mother began to ignore him. "You're so ugly!" they cried.

The ugly duckling was chased this way and that. The other ducks pecked him so much that he ran away from the farm as fast as his little legs could carry him.

The sad little duckling hid in the thick reeds
of the marshes where no one would see him.
Soon, the hunters with fierce dogs came
along, but they did not hurt him. "Even they
think I am too ugly to bite," he said.

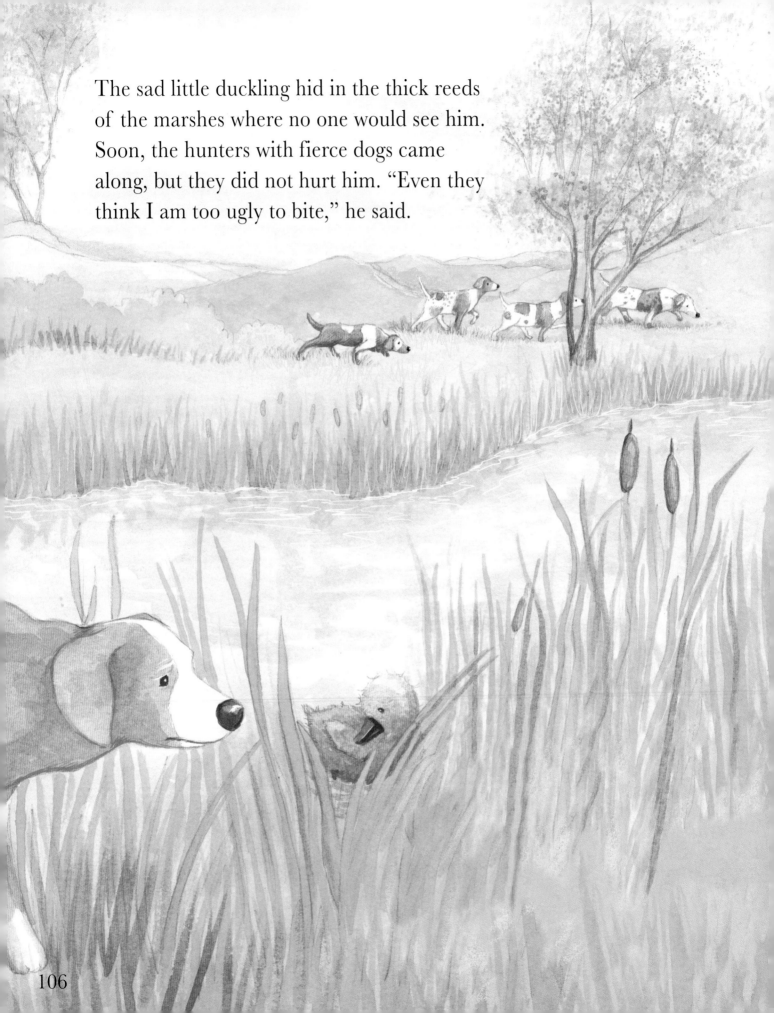

Eventually, the poor little duckling decided to leave the marsh and walk over the fields. He walked a very long way and was hungry and tired, when he came to a little cottage by a wood where an old woman lived. "Come in," she told him, thinking the duckling could lay eggs for her, so she let him stay with her and her pet cat and hen.

For some time, the little duckling was happy in the old woman's cottage. Then, one day, he felt the urge to swim. "No, you mustn't," said the cat and the hen. "You should forget all about swimming and be just like us."

The ugly duckling couldn't purr like the cat, or cluck like the hen. "I don't belong here after all," he thought, sadly, and so he left the little cottage.

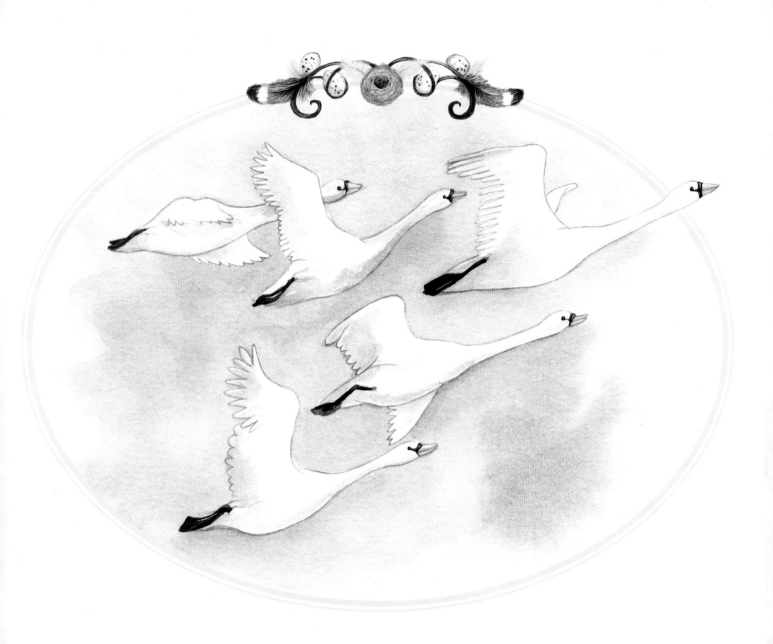

The ugly little duckling returned to the river where he belonged, and he swam and dived, as his family had. The other animals avoided him because of his ugliness and he was very lonely. One day, a flock of beautiful, white birds flew across the sky. Their dazzling beauty made the ugly duckling's heart leap and a longing stirred in him that he could not explain, but he had no one to tell.

Soon, the bitter cold of winter fell upon the land. The reeds and river froze and the ugly duckling was trapped by ice and snow. Luckily for him, a kind man was passing by. He pulled the shivering duckling from the ice and took him home. "Look what I found in the river," the man said to his children. The man set the duckling down by the fire and the heat made him feel warm and safe.

The man's children were very excited. They wanted to play with the ugly duckling, but the poor creature was very afraid. He flapped his wings, as the children chased him around.

First, the ugly duckling upset the milk bucket, then he knocked into a sack of corn. "Stop! Stop!" screeched the man's wife. The poor duckling was so frightened, he ran out through the open door, into the falling snow.

Somehow, the ugly duckling survived the long, dark winter and, when spring came, all of the frozen ponds melted with the first rays of sunshine. The ugly duckling was still sad and longed for a friend, so he approached a crystal clear pond and saw a family of the most beautiful birds. He remembered seeing them once before and suddenly, one of them glided gracefully over to the ugly duckling. He waited for their first cruel words, just as he had come to expect from all the other creatures he had met.

"My, my!" said the graceful swan. "Your feathers are the whitest I have ever seen. How they gleam in the sun!" Confused, the ugly duckling looked down in the rippling water and saw his own reflection.

Much to his surprise, it wasn't that of a grey, ugly duckling, but a graceful, gleaming swan. At last, he had found where he belonged. Never again would he be seen as the ugly duckling, for now he was truly a beautiful swan.

Hans Christian Andersen

The Emperor's New Clothes

Long ago, there lived an emperor who loved nothing more than dressing up in fine, expensive clothes. "Bring me more!" he would say, for as soon as he had bought one thing, he just wanted another. The greedy emperor never gave a single thought to the people who lived in his kingdom. All he cared about was spending their taxes on new clothes for himself.

Then, one day, two mysterious men arrived in the kingdom. They told everyone that they were weavers from a faraway land who could make the most incredible cloth. "This cloth is not only beautiful," they said, "but to anyone who is foolish, the cloth will appear invisible." What the townspeople didn't know was that the weavers were a pair of swindlers.

Before long, the emperor himself came to hear about the swindlers'
magical cloth. "I want to see these weavers, immediately," he commanded
his servants. "With this cloth, not only will I have the most elegant clothes
in all the land," he thought, "but I can find out which of my subjects are
the most foolish!" No sooner had the emperor commanded it, than the
swindlers arrived at his grand palace.

"We promise to make you the finest suit you have ever worn," they said, bowing low to the emperor, with a grin. They were given money, silk and the most expensive golden thread to make their incredible cloth.

The cunning pair used none of the things they had been given, but kept it all for themselves, instead. They sat at two empty spinning wheels and pretended to work until long into the night.

Soon, the vain emperor became impatient to see his beautiful new suit. Then, suddenly, he began to worry. "Wait... what if I can't see it?" he realised. "My subjects will think I'm foolish and too stupid to rule them!" So, the clever emperor sent his most trusted advisor to see if the cloth was ready, instead.

"Here is the magical cloth," said the swindlers to the advisor, pointing to the empty spinning wheel.

"Can't you see the beautiful fabric?" they asked, with a twinkle in their eyes. The advisor peered long and hard. Then he frowned, for of course, there was nothing there to see. However, he was so worried about appearing foolish, that he pretended he could see the cloth, exactly as the swindlers had described. "Oh, yes. It is the finest, most beautiful cloth I have ever seen!" he cried.

After that, the emperor decided to see the cloth for himself. The swindlers convinced him, too, of its beauty.

The emperor, fearing he might be thought very stupid, said, "Oh, yes, it is indeed the finest cloth I have ever seen. It is so fine that, once my suit is made, I wish to wear it in a parade through the whole kingdom."

So, the two swindlers
pretended to cut the
invisible cloth.

Then, they pretended to sew
it with needles with no thread.
Soon, they announced that
the special suit was ready.

"Here are the trousers," they said. "Here is the
coat and a cloak, too." The swindlers handed the
invisible suit around to the emperor's courtiers.
"Feel how light it is," they said. "It is the most
incredible cloth you will ever see. It is even lighter
than air."

123

The courtiers all agreed, for they too were afraid to say that they could see nothing at all. "Could we ask you to undress, Your Majesty," asked the swindlers, "so that we can fit your new suit and show everyone how marvellous you look in it?" All the courtiers looked on as the emperor took off his clothes and stood in his underwear.

Meanwhile, the swindlers pretended to put on all the pieces of the new suit. "How fine you look!" cried the courtiers. "How wonderfully it fits, Your Majesty!"

The emperor looked at his reflection in the mirror. He saw nothing but his underwear, but because he was too afraid to say anything, for fear of being judged as foolish, he simply smiled and said, "I am ready for my parade."

With that, the emperor led the way outside into the streets of the town. The people of the kingdom had heard all about the emperor's incredible new suit and that if they could not see it, they must be very stupid. So, there was much cheering and clapping as they saw the emperor approaching.

"What a marvellous suit!" they cried.
"How well it fits him!" Not a single person
wished the other to know that, in fact, they
could see nothing at all. Suddenly, a little boy stood
out from the crowd. He pointed up at the emperor and
said, "Look, Mother. He's only wearing his pants!"

The crowd went quiet and the little boy spoke again. "Mother," he said, "the emperor is parading through the town in his underwear!" The little boy began to laugh. The emperor looked down at himself. At first, he looked puzzled. Then, he looked annoyed. After a while, however, he too began to laugh.

Before long, everyone was laughing. The emperor realised that he had
been tricked by the swindlers, but he wasn't cross. "What a proud and
foolish man I have been," he said. "Forgive me, my loyal subjects."
After that, the emperor put his real clothes on and commanded that
everyone should have a great big party.

~ Hans Christian Andersen ~

The Nightingale

Long ago, there was a Chinese emperor who had everything he could have ever wished for. He had all the riches in the world, as well as banquets every day and servants to wait on him hand and foot. Everyone marvelled at his white, marble palace, which stood in beautiful gardens that were so large, even the gardener did not know where they ended.

One day, when the emperor was walking among the sweet-smelling flowers, he heard the most beautiful sound he had ever heard. It was a birdsong so soothing and gentle, it sounded like the voice of an angel. The emperor was entranced. "I must have that bird for myself," he said, so he summoned his servants straight away.

The servants asked everyone in the palace where they could find the singing bird. Not one person had heard of it, until they found a maid working in the kitchen. "Yes, I know it," she answered. "It is a nightingale. I have often heard it in the woods when I visit my mother."

She agreed to help the servants find it and they set off that very evening.

They had not been searching long, when suddenly, they heard mooing. "That must be the beautiful song the emperor heard," declared one servant.

"No," laughed the kitchen maid, "that's a cow!" Soon after, they heard a loud croaking.

"There it is!" exclaimed another. "No," said the kitchen maid, "that's a frog!" Then, a bird began to sing a beautiful tune. "Listen.. that's the nightingale!" cried the kitchen maid.

Everyone looked up and there, high on a branch, was a small, brown bird. Though it looked plain and ordinary, its song was just as sweet as the emperor had promised. "Beautiful nightingale," asked the maid, "will you come and sing for the emperor?"

"Gladly," answered the kind nightingale, and she flew down and sat on the maid's hand. They led her back to the palace and the emperor was delighted. "Now I can listen to the nightingale's beautiful song whenever I please," he beamed.

The emperor never tired of listening to the nightingale. She made him so happy that he ordered the servants to attach a long, golden thread to the nightingale's foot so she would always be with him. The nightingale longed for her freedom, but continued to sing her beautiful song.

Then one day, the emperor received a very special present. It was a small, jewelled box and inside was a mechanical bird. It was made from gold and covered with precious stones that twinkled and gleamed.

137

When the emperor wound up the dazzling, mechanical bird, he found that it sang without stopping. "I think I prefer this bird to the nightingale," said the emperor. "The nightingale looks plain, but this new, mechanical bird is so bright and beautiful. I want to look at it all the time!" So, the emperor untied the golden thread which held the nightingale and, with a sad heart, the little bird flew away.

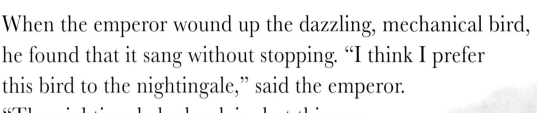

Just as the nightingale once had, the new mechanical bird made the emperor very happy. This time, however, he was happy for many years longer. Then, one morning, something unexpected happened. The singing suddenly stopped.

"It just needs winding up!" the emperor said to his servant. He wound up the bird, but nothing happened. "Do it again," ordered the emperor. The servant did as he said, but it was no use. The mechanical bird was broken.

The emperor was very upset. He paced up and down the room. "What will I do?" he cried. "I cannot live without the song of the bird to comfort me." As the days went by, the emperor became more and more sad. Before long, he became ill and didn't even get up to eat. His servants were very worried. "He may never get better," they whispered to each other.

Then, one of the emperor's servants had an idea. "We must find the real nightingale. We can ask if she will come back to the palace and sing to the emperor again," he said. "It is the only way to save him!"

Strangely enough, when the servants found the nightingale in the palace gardens, she seemed to be waiting for them. The servant explained what had happened. "Please, will you come back?" he asked, humbly.

"I'll be glad to," said the kind, forgiving nightingale, "but I have one request. I will sing to the emperor as often as he wishes, as long as I can remain free to come and go as I please."

The emperor agreed, so the nightingale perched on a branch outside his bedroom window and began to sing. The emperor lay in his bed and listened, then slowly, he began to feel better.

"How could I ever have preferred the mechanical bird to this beautiful creature?" he thought. "The real nightingale is far better, no matter how she looks." There were great celebrations in the palace when the emperor was completely well again and the servants arranged a grand feast for the whole kingdom. The nightingale was the guest of honour and, for many years afterwards, the emperor lived a long and happy life with her at his side.

Hans Christian Andersen

Thumbelina

There once was a woman who wanted a child more than anything in the world. One day, the woman was in her garden when she saw a beautiful rosebud. She made her wish for a child out loud and suddenly, as if by magic, the petals opened. Inside the rose was a tiny girl. She was barely the size of a thumb, so the delighted woman decided to call her Thumbelina. A walnut shell was her cradle and a rose leaf was her cosy bedspread. She slept peacefully there every night and Thumbelina made the woman happy.

Then, one night, a big, ugly toad crept in through the window of the woman's house and took Thumbelina away. "You will make a pretty wife for my son," said the toad, and he left Thumbelina on a lily pad, while he hopped off to find his son.

Thumbelina looked around at the deep water and felt very afraid. Then, suddenly, she saw lots of fish poking their heads up from below the water. "A pretty girl like you shouldn't have to marry an ugly toad!" they cried, so they nibbled at the roots of the lily until it began to float downstream.

The lily pad drifted along on the water. As the sun came up, the water glittered like gold. "How pretty it is," thought Thumbelina. She felt very glad that she had escaped from that ugly toad once and for all.

149

Just then, a yellow butterfly fluttered past. Thumbelina quickly tied some ribbon from her dress to its feet and the butterfly pulled the lily pad even faster downstream.

Thumbelina was just beginning to enjoy the many things she saw on the riverbank when, suddenly, a huge beetle swooped down and grabbed her by the waist. It lifted her off the lily pad and flew off with her into the trees.

Little Thumbelina was very frightened and became even more so when she saw all the other beetles in the tree. "What is this you have brought to us?" they asked, laughing. "It is rather ugly and looks like a tiny human. We have no use for such a strange-looking creature."

The beetle who had grabbed Thumbelina did not wish to upset his family. "I have no use for you either, little creature," he said and, grabbing Thumbelina once again, he flew out of the tree and set her down near a patch of daisies in the forest. Poor Thumbelina cried and cried, for she did not want to be thought of as ugly.

All summer long, Thumbelina lived alone.
She slept in a bed made of leaves under a
big, broad green leaf. She scooped nectar
from the flowers and drank dew from the
morning grass.

Too soon, however, winter came. The sharp frost chilled Thumbelina's bones and she shivered with cold. "I must leave this place," she said, "or I shall surely freeze to death."

So, Thumbelina set off. A little way beyond the forest, she came across a meadow in which a field mouse lived.

153

The field mouse's little house
looked snug and warm. It smelled
richly of delicious roasting nuts.
Thumbelina was so hungry, she
knocked on the door of the little
house and asked if she could come in.

The field mouse was very kind
to Thumbelina. "If you clean for me
and tell me stories, I will give you a
home," he said. So, Thumbelina
worked happily for the field mouse.

She even made friends with an injured swallow who had nearly perished in the cold. She wrapped him up warmly and fed him until the spring came and he was able to fly free once more.

Thumbelina was very happy until, one day, a mole came to call at the house. He was a bossy, grumpy creature who, at one glance, fell in love with Thumbelina and decided to marry her. He wanted her to live in his underground home, so she would never see the sunshine again. Thumbelina was terribly upset. "What will I do?" she asked the spring flowers and the trees. "Even the field mouse wants me to marry the mole. If only my swallow friend was here to help me."

Suddenly, there was a twittering from the trees. "Here I am," said the swallow. "Jump on my back, Thumbelina, and we will fly far away from here." Thumbelina was overjoyed to see her friend. She quickly jumped on his back and they flew, up, up into the blue sky.

The bird flew far away with Thumbelina, over fields and trees, until they reached a lush forest where the most beautiful white flowers grew. The swallow set Thumbelina down on one of the flowers and said, "This will be your home, now."

The tiny girl was so astonished when suddenly, she saw the petals of
a nearby flower open to reveal a tiny man, no bigger than herself!
He had a gold crown on his head and he smiled at Thumbelina.
She was enchanted by him and thought he was very handsome.

"I am King of the Flowers," said the little man, smiling. He, in turn, was enchanted by Thumbelina. "Will you be my queen?" he asked.

"Of course," said Thumbelina, for she had fallen instantly in love with him. There was much rejoicing and, high in the trees, the little swallow sang his happy song, as Thumbelina became the beautiful queen of all the flowers.

Hans Christian Andersen

The Tinderbox

Once upon a time, a young soldier was making his very long journey home. "Who are you?" he asked, when he came across a strange-looking woman. She wore a cape and the skin on her face was rough, like the bark of an old tree. "Young man," she asked, softly, "would you like to make your fortune?" The soldier frowned, but he was poor and hungry after his time at war. "What would I have to do?" he asked, growing curious. "You see that hollow tree?" she asked, pointing. "At the bottom are three doors. Inside each is a room full of treasure, guarded by a fierce dog." Then, she gave the soldier her apron. "Lay this down for each of the dogs to sit on," she said, "and you will see that they will instantly become as sweet as puppies." The old woman told the soldier that all she wanted in return was for him to bring her an old tinderbox that her grandmother had left down the hollow tree.

The soldier couldn't refuse the old woman's offer and quickly climbed down inside the tree. When he gently pushed open the first door, he couldn't believe his eyes.

Sitting in front of a treasure chest filled with copper coins was a huge, snarling dog. "Your eyes are as big as teacups," whispered the soldier, laying down the woman's apron.

Just as she'd promised, the dog instantly calmed, so the soldier filled his pack and tiptoed away.

Next, the soldier went to the second door and carefully peered inside. Sure enough, what he saw was even worse than before. There were two eyes, as big as saucers, staring at him and he heard the SNAP, SNAPPING of the dog's jaws. "I must get to the chest," thought the soldier, as he laid down the apron. As soon as the dog was quiet, the soldier helped himself to the treasure once more.

When the soldier opened the third door, he was met with the sight of the fiercest dog of all. The dog towered over the chest he guarded, which overflowed with bright, golden coins and his eyes were as big as dinner plates. "Good dog," said the soldier, nervously, putting down the blue apron and creeping past him. As he gathered up the treasure for the final time, he spied the old woman's tinderbox and carefully placed it in his pocket, as she'd asked.

When the soldier was ready to be pulled back up the tree, the old woman called, "Do you have my tinderbox?" When he appeared at the top, she did not greet him so pleasantly.

Instead, she shrieked, "GIVE ME MY TINDERBOX!" She grabbed at the soldier with her crooked hands and sharp nails.

Quickly, the soldier drew his sword and before his eyes, the old woman disappeared in a flash.

Finally rid of the old woman, the soldier journeyed home with his treasure. He bought fine clothes and held luxurious dinner parties with the richest gentlemen of the land.

Very soon, the soldier had nothing left, not even enough to light a fire. "What's this?" he wondered, suddenly finding the old woman's tinderbox.

He struck it once and the dog with eyes as big as teacups magically appeared in front of him.

"Could it be that the tinderbox summons magical dogs who will grant my every wish?" thought the soldier. "Bring me a bag of copper coins," he commanded. Then, the dog reappeared instantly, dropping the coins at his feet. So, the soldier struck the tinderbox twice and, this time, the dog with eyes as big as saucers appeared. Finally, he struck the tinderbox three times and the dog with eyes as big as dinner plates joined the group. Each one brought him more riches than the last.

The soldier went back to enjoying his life of luxury with his new-found riches. "You should marry the princess!" exclaimed a rich gentleman one night. The soldier was very lonely and was desperate to hear more. "When the king's daughter was born," said the gentleman, "a wise woman told him she would marry a commoner. So, the angry king keeps the princess locked in her room, so that she will never mix with ordinary people."

"I must rescue the poor princess," thought the soldier. So, that night, he summoned the dog with eyes as big as teacups. "Go to the palace and bring the princess to me," he said, "so that we might fall in love." WOOF! replied the dog, as he leapt from the soldier's room to rescue the princess. He flew over the kingdom with the sleeping princess on his back and she and the soldier spent the whole night talking and laughing. At dawn, the dog carried the princess back to her own room in the palace.

The next morning, the princess told the king she'd had a strange dream. "A huge dog carried me to a handsome soldier's room and we had a lovely time together," she told him.

The king rightly suspected that it wasn't a dream at all. So, that night, when the soldier sent the second dog for the princess, he had a servant follow them. "Mark whichever door they enter with a chalk cross," instructed the king.

When the soldier saw the cross on the door the next morning, he guessed the king had sent someone to follow the princess. "Ha!" he said, "You won't catch me that easily, Your Majesty."

So, he commanded one of the dogs to go outside and mark every house in the whole kingdom with a chalk cross on its door. When the king's men came for him, they were very puzzled indeed!

Next, it was the queen's turn to come up with a plan. "Take this silk purse," she told a servant, after filling it with flour and making a hole in it. "Tie it around the princess' waist while she is asleep."

The servant did as she was told and, when the third dog took the princess back to the soldier's room that night, a trail of white flour was left behind for the king's men to follow.

This time, the plan worked. The king's men arrested the soldier and flung him into a damp, dark prison. "My dear, sweet princess," sobbed the soldier, as he sat in the darkness, all alone. "I shall never see her again." Then, he remembered his tinderbox. He struck it once, then twice, then three times, until all three magical dogs appeared before his eyes. "Help me escape, at once!" he commanded.

The three dogs leapt to obey their master. Growling and snapping, they chased the king and queen out of the land, never to be seen again. Free at last, the soldier and the princess were married before the whole kingdom. Of course, the guests of honour at the wedding feast were the dog with eyes as big as teacups, the dog with eyes as big as saucers and the dog with eyes as big as dinner plates. They all lived together, happily ever after.